# God Made It All

by Mary Thornton Blanton
illustrated by
Helen Endres

Published by The Dandelion House
A Division of The Child's World

for distribution by  VICTOR ─────────

BOOKS a division of SP Publications, Inc.

WHEATON ILLINOIS 60187

Offices also in
Whitby, Ontario, Canada
Amersham-on-the-Hill, Bucks, England

Published by The Dandelion House, A Division of The Child's World, Inc.
© 1983 SP Publications, Inc. All rights reserved. Printed in U.S.A.

A Book for Preschoolers.

**Library of Congress Cataloging in Publication Data**

Blanton, Mary Thornton, 1926-
  God made it all!

  Summary: Mentions many of the things in our world
which were made by God and for which we are grateful.
    1. Creation—Juvenile literature.   [1. God.
2. Creation]   I. Endres, Helen, ill.   II. Title.
BS651.B55  1983                231.7'65                83-7345
ISBN 0-89693-209-5

1 2 3 4 5 6 7 8 9 10 11 12 R 90 89 88 87 86 85 84 83

# God Made It All

"God saw all that he had
made, and it was very good."
—Genesis 1:31 (NIV)

# Who made the flowers that bloom . . .

in spring?

God did.

Who made the birds
and gave them wings?

God did.

Who made bunnies . . .

and
frogs . . .

and
ducklings too?

9

Who made the
animals in the
zoo?

God did!

Who made the sunshine?

# Who made the snow?

Who made the rain . . .

and the bright rainbow?

God did!

Who made the ocean?
Who made the sand?
Who made the shells
I hold in my hand?

God did.

Who made the moon
and the stars
in the skies?

Who made the apples . . .

. . . for apple pies?

God did!

Who made the strawberries
for strawberry jam?

Who made
the sheep . . .

. . . and the wooly lamb?

Who made all the food
we eat each day?

Who made the acorns . . .

. . . the squirrels store away?

God did.

Who made
my friends?

Who made me?

And who was it that made
my family? It was God.

For God made all things.

The Lord is a great God. . .
The sea is His, and He made it!
And His hands formed the dry land.
Know that the Lord, He is God.
It is He that has made us.
For the Lord is good.
　　　　—*Selected from Psalms 95 and 100*

# Who Started Everything?